The Enormous Suitcase

Robert Munsch

illustrated by
Michael Martchenko

North Winds Press
An Imprint of Scholastic Canada Ltd.

The art for this book was painted in watercolour on Crescent illustration board.
The type is set in 24 point Perpetua Regular.

Library and Archives Canada Cataloguing in Publication

Munsch, Robert N., 1945-, author
The enormous suitcase / by Robert Munsch ; illustrated
by Michael Martchenko.

ISBN 978-1-4431-6317-0 (hardcover)

I. Martchenko, Michael, illustrator II. Title.

PS8576.U575E56 2017   jC813'.54   C2017-903045-0

www.scholastic.ca

6 5 4 3 2 1   Printed in Canada 114   17 18 19 20 21

For Kelsey Roach Stolo, and
Alexander and Rowan Stolo,
Calgary, Alberta.
— *R.M.*

When it was time to go to her
dad's house, Kelsey opened her
suitcase and put in clean clothes,
a big box of coloured pencils, three
books and her unicorn picture.

"You're taking the picture right off the wall?" said her mom.

"Yes," said Kelsey. "I like this picture. I think *I* should live in one house and both of *you* should visit *me,* but that is not going to happen, so I am taking my picture back and forth."

"Well . . . okay," said her mom.

Then Kelsey and her mom drove
over to her dad's house.

When Kelsey got there, she pounded a nail into the wall so she could put the unicorn picture above her bed.

A week later, when it was time to go back to her mom's house, Kelsey opened her suitcase and put in clean clothes, a big box of coloured pencils, four books, her unicorn picture and a pillow.

"A pillow?" said her dad. "Your mom has lots of pillows."

"I know," said Kelsey. "But I like this pillow best."

Then Kelsey and her dad drove
over to her mom's house.

A week later, when it was time to go back to her dad's house, Kelsey opened her suitcase and put in clean clothes, a big box of coloured pencils, five books, her unicorn picture, her pillow and her mom's pet dog.

"Whoa!" said her mom. "Not the dog. You definitely can't take the dog."

But as soon as her mom left the room, Kelsey put the dog back in her suitcase and went out to catch the bus.

The bus driver said, "WOW! That's an enormous suitcase! You must be going far."

"No," said Kelsey, "I am just going to my dad's house. I am taking the bus because my mom said I could not bring the dog with me. But I did bring the dog, so I am taking the bus."

Then Kelsey opened her suitcase and took out the dog.

"Yikes," yelled the driver. "No dogs on the bus!"

But everybody on the bus yelled,
"GIVE THE KID A BREAK!"

So the driver let Kelsey keep the dog on the bus, as long as Kelsey promised to keep it on her lap.

When Kelsey got off the bus, she dragged her suitcase to her dad's house and knocked.

Her dad opened the door and said, "Hi, Kelsey. How come your mom let you bring the dog?"

Just then her dad's phone rang. Kelsey grabbed it and said, "Hi!"

"KELSEY!" yelled her mom. "I did not know where you were. Are you safe? How did you get to your dad's?"

"It's okay, Mom," said Kelsey. "I took the bus because I had to bring the dog. I always miss the dog."

"But Kelsey," said her mom, "your dad has a cat. The dog will eat the cat!"

"Yikes!" said Kelsey. "I forgot about the cat!" and she hung up and ran to get the dog before it ate the cat.

But when she got there, the dog was asleep on the floor and the cat was asleep on the dog.

"Neat!" said Kelsey. "They get along."

"Yes," said Kelsey's dad. "Isn't it amazing how things can work out if you just try?"

"Yes," said Kelsey, and she gave her dad a big hug.

So the next time Kelsey went to her dad's, she took her goldfish.

But the cat ate the goldfish.
Because it turns out that some
things just do not work out, no
matter how hard you try.